For Jazz & Jess, live your best lives - Julia
To Zaila & Samir, love you - Lily

Published in the United Kingdom by:

Blue Falcon Publishing
The Mill, Pury Hill Business Park,
Alderton Road, Towcester
Northamptonshire NN12 7LS
Email: books@bluefalconpublishing.co.uk
Web: www.bluefalconpublishing.co.uk

A CIP record of this book is available from the British Library.

First printed October 2021
ISBN 9781912765393

Frederick the frog said,
"I think I'm a duck!

I'm small with soft feathers,
a beak and I cluck!"

But the other frogs croaked...

They all laughed.

"Your skin is so slimy,

your jump is real high,

your eyes are like bugs

and you really can't fly."

Fred felt quite angry and Fred felt quite bad.

He jumped up and on to a green lily pad.

"If you're a duck, Fred, then give us a quack, give us a quack and we'll listen right back."

Fred quacked and he quacked with a big smiley grin:
"I know I'm a duck, I just want to fit in."

But the other frogs croaked...

They all laughed.

"Your skin is so slimy,

your jump is real high,

your eyes are like bugs

and you really can't fly."

Fred felt unhappy, Fred felt in a muddle.

He jumped from the lily pad, into a puddle.

"If you're a duck, Fred, then swim like a duck. Swim like a duck in that puddle of muck."

Fred swam like a duck in the puddle of muck.
He swam and he swam until he got stuck.

And the other frogs croaked...

They all laughed.

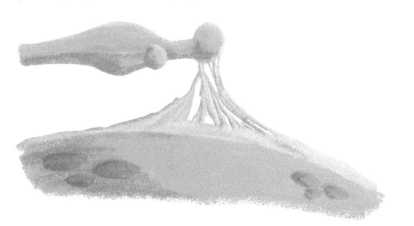

"Your skin is so slimy,

your jump is real high,

your eyes are like bugs

and you really can't fly."

Fred felt quite lonely and Fred felt quite sad.

He went home to talk to his mum and his dad.

"I think I'm a duck!"
And he croaked out a quack.

His parents, they smiled
as they stroked his cold back.

"If you feel like a duck in your body, dear Fred, then a duck you shall be. It's your life!" They both said.

So Fred left his home, waddling straight to the frogs.

I've got some good news!

They all jumped off their logs.

"Look, frogs, it's true, you can be how you feel,
live as you wish, and it's not a big deal.

It's not what you look like,
or how you behave,
it's the feeling inside and
the strength to be brave."

The frogs, they took stock
of what Frederick had said.
They understood why
he would waddle instead.

"Fred, we were wrong,
we're so sorry, it's true:
you are the most wonderful duck
through and through."

CPSIA information can be obtained
at www.ICGtesting.com
Printed in the USA
BVHW051015261021
619918BV00005B/174

9 781912 765393